MARPLE'S Arples

Marple's Arples
Copyright © 2024 by George; Judy Ennis

ISBN: 979-8895310380 (hc)
ISBN: 979-8895310366 (sc)
ISBN: 979-8895310373 (e)

All rights reserved. No part of this publication may be reproduced, distributed, or transmitted in any form or by any means, including photocopying, recording, or other electronic or mechanical methods, without the prior written permission of the publisher and/or the author, except in the case of brief quotations embodied in critical reviews and other noncommercial uses permitted by copyright law.

The views expressed in this book are solely those of the author and do not necessarily reflect the views of the publisher, and the publisher hereby disclaims any responsibility for them.

Writers' Branding
(877) 608-6550
www.writersbranding.com
media@writersbranding.com

MARPLE'S
Arples

GEORGE; JUDY ENNIS

I would like to dedicate this book to my

wife who is a terrific typist.

MARPLE'S ARPLES

-Sarah, take Posey and go down to Marple's Arples and pick a bushel of apples.

-I was just on my way to Rachel's.

-Well, then you can just take Rachel with you, mind, a whole bushel.

-What if she doesn't want to go?

-Child, your mother and I have four pies to bake for Maundy Thursday. We all must do the Lord's work. Now git!

-Yes, Grandma.

As Sarah got older, she found herself more and more at odds with the forces for good. Mom had Grandma and Grandma had God. So she obediently took her little sister and went to Rachel's.

Mrs. Wade was delighted to offer her Rachel for such a worthy cause, and she recruited Jenny-May from next door. So the four girls, carrying two bushels between them, made the trip to Marple's Arples.

There was never a more perfect day to pick apples. The sun shone bright and warm. A pesky breeze blew against their skirts, and bugs crawled, jumped and flew. The birds preened their bright feathers as if grooming for a magnificent feast. The call of nature was in every creature.

The ancient orchard with its great outstretched arms was heavy with red, swollen apples, but they were out of reach. and the branches were high up and difficult to negotiate, especially in long, full dresses. The girls fretted and complained about the chores their mothers made them do.

Just then pebbles rolled past them on the ground, then one struck Rachel's skirt. She had known enough boys to realize what pests they could be. She quickly sized up the situation.

-Wilbur Jackson, you come out of there. You're so scared of girls you hide behind bushes!

Wilbur Jackson quickly emerged from behind a pile of dead branches. He was stung by her remark and did not want to appear like a scaredy-cat when confronted by the fair sex. With him was a new boy who had just moved in. The two boys grinned and sat down under the biggest tree and began to eat apples.

-How'd you know it was me?

-Wilbur, it's all over school that you sneak up on girls.

-…be obliged if you called me Will.

Sarah saw an end to their dilemma and sweetly asked the boys if they would help pick apples, adding that they were so much bigger and stronger.

-We'll pick all the apples on this here tree, if you give us a kiss.

The ladies, duly shocked and horrified, upbraided the youths and lectured them on manners, but they did not refuse. Rachel fussed and fumed like a angry hen:

-Wilbur, you're too scrawny to even get on that first limb.

This time Rachel's challenge did not work Wilbur was not at all compelled to prove himself. The two boys grinned ear to ear and smirked, realizing in triumph that they had landed four pretty birds. The boys laughed as if it were all a funny joke, but their hearts pounded in anticipation, for the capricious breeze played with the girls' long tresses and blew against their skirts, outlining their youth.

The four young ladies looked at the two farm boys. They were not Disciples of Christ, but they did go to the Baptist tent and river meetings.

Their sun-bleached hair fell over handsome features, and by their large brown forearms you could tell they had on-loaded hay for more than one fall.

Then Posey, much to Sarah's disapproval, looked way up into the branches and said wistfully: 'Those branches are mighty high!

Sarah was scandalized by the confession of her little sister and pushed her away from the boys.

-You can't kiss Posey; she's only twelve.

Posey reacted angrily and lashed out at Sarah with the venom of a viper. She kicked her older sister on the side of her foot.

-You do your own courting', y'old ninny!

Sarah was bewildered by Posey's outburst, when she tried to protect her. The boys began laughing. Sarah didn't like it when people laughed at her family. In hurt and anger she yelled at the boys:

-Kissing isn't done like that.

Then Rachel flew at Sarah.

-Now, you've spoiled everything. We could have been home in an hour with two bushels all cuz you don't like boys!

Sarah turned her back and departed before the tears streamed down her face. She just kept going. She was shocked when her friends and little sister turned on her.

Sarah kept walking and after awhile it made her feel better. She settled down to a steady gate and looked for a good road home.

She would tell her mother that they fought, and there were no apples. Her mother would tell Grandma, and Grandma would … The poor girl groaned. She was already being punished, but she walked on bravely, determined to make her own peace with God.

She heard the sound of a cantering horse behind her. She turned around to see a horse and rider coming up fast on her. He came out of the setting sun, and she shielded her eyes trying to see who it was.

The rider reined in not fifteen feet from Sarah and then circled her at a trot. It was an army officer on the biggest Appaloosa she had ever seen. Appys were Sarah's favorite horse because they reminded her of Uncle Ned. The man held out a big leather gloved hand to her, and without a care or thought in her head, Sarah grabbed his hand with both of hers and put her toe between his boot and stirrup strap. One mighty tug and she was up seated across the front of his saddle sitting with him sidesaddle in the circle of his arms. His dark blue uniform was accented by two gold bars on his shoulders and a gold saber at his side. He smiled at her with a warm, confident smile. He quite literally swept Sarah off her feet.

They were off in a slow, easy lope. She felt as light as a feather and had not a care in the world where they were going. He had a closely trimmed mustache and sad, intelligent eyes. He had lost comrades, she thought, and had probably been shot at and even wounded. She was totally possessed by his sad smile, and she smiled back at him and trusted him like her own family.

The ride ended much too soon when Sarah found herself not at home but back at Marple's Arples. There in view of the boys and girls she just fled, the officer kissed her full upon the mouth, and then set her down on the ground. The girls gasped in disbelief. Rachel wondered if Sarah planned the whole thing to get even . The boys agonized realizing they had been bested by the army.

The officer dismounted, gave the reins to Sarah and sprang into the venerable old tree and shook its limbs so hard that apples came thumping down everywhere, making the kids run for cover.

Sarah watched her friends and the beautiful red rain of apples, but it seemed very far away and slowed down to almost a standstill. Her thought went inward for she was very aware that she had been kissed by a man. She felt all right. She really didn't permit it, but he was so close. It seemed the simplest, most natural thing to do.

The old tree gave up its fruit, and the girls ran underneath and excitedly gathered the apples. The boys proved good sports and helped out. But Sarah stood motionless. The kiss grew and grew inside her soul.

Her heart pounded when she realized he might want another when he came back to collect his horse. What should she do? She was most afraid of betraying the shyness and awkwardness of her youth. Questions tumbled in her head, and she had no answers. One kiss could be explained, but not two. People would talk. Mom would find out, and she would tell Grandma. Then Sarah beheld the Garden of Eden and remembered that all mankind's sins began under an apple tree. She had no time to struggle with good and evil for her cavalier was returning for his horse. Sarah prayed for composure. In the last moment she resolved not to retreat in fear or run up to him in eagerness. When he was close, she stood up straight, smiled and waited. He handed her the biggest, reddest apple she'd ever seen, remounted, and rode away at a gallop.

www.ingramcontent.com/pod-product-compliance
Lightning Source LLC
LaVergne TN
LVHW070445070526
838199LV00036B/695